newborn

NEWBORN

or

Now the Green Blade Rises

Agustín Maes

Whisk(e)y Tit
NYC & VT

Published in the United States by Whisk(e)y Tit: www.whiskeytit.com. If you wish to use or reproduce all or part of this book for any means, please let the author and publisher know. You're pretty much required to, legally.

ISBN 978-1-7329596-5-1

Library of Congress Control Number: 2019953612

Cover design by Jessica Cadkin.

First Whisk(e)y Tit paperback edition.

For Jessica

La beauté du monde est l'orifice du labyrinthe.

— Simone Weil

Shafts of afternoon light rained through oak and willow and eucalyptus, the boys' small faces stippled with fine golden sunspots as though behind lacework mourning veils knitted from shadow. They stood side-by-side at the edge of a broad yawn of creekbed, eyes bound to what they had discovered there amongst sedge and blackberry and wild rye. Neither spoke. But for birdsong and the muted hum of cars along the nearby avenue it was quiet, the creek gurgling softly in its summer-thinned course. A mizzle of sunbeams shone across the water in fingernail crescents, quick lustrous flashes where an overturned shopping cart formed a mounded swell. The boys remained in fainter light, motionless beside the small still pool of an inlet shaded by the steep bank's tangle of tree roots. Water skimmers skated over the pond's glassy surface, the insects' needle-thin legs dimpling the youngsters' reflections and the

1

reflection of the infant at their feet, its image little more than a wavering smudge.

"Jesus," one of them whispered.

The other boy, the one who had seen it first, said nothing, turning away to face the creek.

Strands of algae undulated from the corroded lattice of the shopping cart, caster wheels cocked and rust-frozen above the riffling water like the hooves of some drowned mechanical bovine through whose bones the stream sluiced. He lifted his gaze to the opposite bank, its network of intertwined roots and gangling blackberry canes counterpart to those of the bank on which he stood, the creek between running in a sun-sparked murmur over loamy silt and smooth-worn stones; a constant thing, ceaseless and certain.

The creek begins three miles west of the town's most westerly house. There at its headwaters stands a dam built in 1951 to reduce the stream's flooding and create a drinking water reservoir maintained by the county. An island pokes from its center, once the top of a hill like the oak-blanketed slopes that wreath the submerged valley, grasses changing with the seasons from summer-parched gold to a green the color of sea glass and back again.

Along the reservoir's shores are a public golf course and a fire trail and up a sloping grade a two lane road that snakes west toward the Pacific Ocean, the cars of recreational fishermen parked along its gravel turnout on weekend afternoons. A smattering of dilapidated picnic tables dot the rangy grass of an ill-kept picnic area on the reservoir's western shore, lopsided benches and tops scarred by years of cigarette burns, initials and obscenities graven into weather-paled wood by teenagers arriving at night to drink and smoke and laugh and fight and sometimes fuck. The teens come no matter the time of year, no matter the heat or cold, now and then dispersed by sheriff's deputies issuing tickets for underage drinking and illegal campfires, flashlight beams shone into blinking eyes.

Bitsy Eddy sat atop one of the graffiti-incised tables on a warm October evening in 1979, her sneakered feet and those of the boy beside her resting on a bench seat. They sat alone in the calm gloaming, a gauzy swarm of gnats at the shore. The boy nudged slowly closer as the lake darkened to a blue-black mirror rippled by the concentric wavelets of feeding fish, drawing nearer until Bitsy felt his thigh touch hers, her quickened heart beating in her mouth.

She had first seen him five days earlier, Bitsy and her friends standing at the side of a Seven-Eleven after final period, friends who were, like Bitsy, freshmen in their first semester of high school; none particularly pretty or popular, none with any experience with boys. They tittered over a mustachioed figure in the small parking lot that Monday afternoon, he leaning against the side of a white Ford Falcon tall and wiry and wearing a faded black T-shirt, unmoving except to occasionally lift an arm to inhale from a cigarette held smoldering between his fingers, a lean biceps revealed by the pack rolled-up in a rectangular bump in one of his sleeves.

Bitsy and her friends cast furtive glances his way and then spun their heads back into a chittering huddle, taking turns sipping at the straw of the cherry Slurpee they shared. When the boy flicked away the butt of his cigarette and walked toward them the trio fell into abrupt silence and stood straight, surprise on their faces.

"Hey," the boy said. He spoke to Bitsy.

Bitsy shifted the weight of her slender form from one foot to the other. "Hi," she said, her voice small.

"You need a ride home?" The boy gestured casually in the direction of his car, the passenger-side door dented and mottled with spots of gray primer paint.

Bitsy looked toward her two girlfriends in silent panic. The Slurpee had tinted the edges of their mouths red, like traces of lipstick wiped hastily away.

"That's okay," Bitsy said, voice high-pitched. Her face and ears grew hot and she knew that she blushed.

"Sure?" the boy said. He lifted his eyebrows and grinned, teeth big and white and so jaggedly uneven they looked almost canine.

"We have plans," Bitsy lied. She heard a quiet snicker and in her peripheral vision saw Margot nudge Gwynn with an elbow in an effort at shushing her.

The boy made a grunting laugh. "That's cool," he said. "Maybe next time." He winked at Bisty and lingered for a moment and then ambled back to his car. When he backed the sedan out of the parking lot he sounded a brief parting honk that set the girls into a buzzing tattle.

He was there again the next afternoon, leaning against his car just as he had before. Though she had shyly declined his offer the previous day, afterward chastising her friends for not corroborating her excuse, Bitsy stepped away from them and ventured across the small parking lot, feeling the eyes of her gawking acquaintances at her back, the straps of the canvas tote bag she held with both hands moistening by the sweat of her palms. "Hi," she said.

The boy nodded, "Hey."

Bitsy immediately regretted her boldness, turning to look toward Gwynn and Margot who stood in rapt scrutiny of a conversation they could not hear. When she turned back toward the boy he had opened the damaged passenger side door, again offering her a ride. Bitsy accepted, nervously shifting the weight of her tote bag from hand to hand as she got in. He started the car and revved it and then guided them slowly onto Center Road, Bitsy's apprehension transforming into a sensation of triumph when she saw the gaping looks on her friends' faces, the boy punching "shave-and-a-haircut" on the horn as they passed.

He asked about Bitsy's name and she told him it was short for Elizabeth and so the boy had called her Elizabeth rather than her nickname and told her to call him Art. As they drove he told her he was eighteen, that he had graduated the previous June. Bitsy liked the idea that he was older. Old enough to legally be considered a man, she thought. But Arthur Dolcini was in fact barely seventeen to her fourteen, having dropped out of school two years earlier. And though he'd told her that he had an apartment and lived on his own, the truth was that he had been kicked out of his parents' house for beating up his own father, living now with a roommate in a trailer on a cattleman's property, both of them working as unpaid farmhands in lieu of rent.

"Beer in the fridge all the time," he said, looking over at the girl, a tanned forearm draped casually over the top of the steering wheel.

"Right on," Bitsy said, nodding.

The boy cocked his head and let out a gruff laugh and Bisty flushed pink with embarrassment, unsure if the sound he made was one of affirmation or amusement at what she had uttered.

She gave him directions to the complex on Fourth Street where she lived in a one-bedroom apartment with her mother. The boy drove his Falcon halfway up the steep concrete driveway of a two-tiered beige rectangle on the side of a hill, propped in front by skinny steel beams that looked no sturdier than the wooden stilts of a treehouse. He stopped and set the brake and got out and walked around the car, opening the primer-spotted passenger door for her and offering a hand to help her out. Bitsy put her hand in his and Art brought it to his lips, his moustache tickling when he kissed it, looking down at her and smiling a mouthful of crooked, pointy teeth.

Bitsy relived that kiss over the next two days, remembering Art's vaguely sour boy smell, her ride home becoming an event that insinuated itself into nearly all her conversations with Gwynn and Margot, friends both jealous and fascinated. She had hoped to see Art again at the Seven-Eleven and her heart lifted when on the following Friday afternoon he was there. Bitsy's friends gossiped over his presence, wordless when she accepted the boy's offer of yet another ride home, this time with a brash, false confidence meant for them: head turned over her shoulder with a mocking grin as she tossed her tote bag in his car and got in. Art suggested they go the long way and she'd said, simply, "Okay," her ride home becoming an aimless drive through town until Art parked his car at the reservoir's gravel turnout, the hot afternoon of a late Indian summer giving way to sunset.

There at the water's edge day surrendered to night. Art scooted toward Bitsy atop the slanting picnic table on which they sat, the hills and the lake's image of the hills silhouetted by the violet nimbus of a newly departed sun. He sidled slowly closer until his side touched hers, arm curling around her shoulders. And then the warmth of a breathy whisper in her ear: "Elizabeth." She shivered at the tingle of his moustache, looking toward the older boy's face and then looking quickly away again even as he took her chin in the calloused palm of his hand, her eyes toward the reservoir, thinking how the darkened water's depth must be as profound as the love her thrashing teenage heart insisted must surely be true.

The depth of the reservoir varies, dependent on winter rains and the length of the dry summer seasons, striated marks of its pebbled banks a chronicle of the man-made lake's ever-changing shoreline. Five years after Bitsy and Art's time together at the lakeshore the reservoir's 4,500 acres will be drained to allow for repairs to the dam, a slow recession that in time will reveal a six-and-half foot, 125-pound white sturgeon, the primordial-looking leviathan's bony form confirming the many old tales and rumors and first-hand accounts of a monster haunting the lake. The discovery will be covered in local papers that August of 1984, the sturgeon's capture and delivery to the Steinhart Aquarium in San Francisco also reported in brief national news stories. But the decades-old fish will not survive the relocation, its existence in a tank at the aquarium lasting only three days, as though its revelation required that the great creature perish in captivity at the hands of those who had come to know that it truly was; the depths that had sustained the mystery of its being also the source of its life.

In the absence of water the reservoir's mucky floor will be exposed, its surface drying to an arid desert of long cracks and splits and fissures, deeper strata remaining soggy by thirty-three years of saturation. The young will continue to come to the lake despite its emptiness, captivated by golf balls and fishing tackle embedded in the baked gray mud like the artifacts of an ancient civilization. They will be enthralled by the odd wobble of the dry moon surface beneath their feet, strolling on it day and night, stoned or drunk or simply killing time after school just as a gawky red-haired fifteen-year-old had done one late afternoon, bounding in comic imitation of a weightless astronaut over the unsteady earth to the amusement of his friends. The pale freckled boy caught a toe in a wide crack and stumbled down in a sprawling fall and the laughter of his companions grew more boisterous. And when he lifted himself up, his face and chest and legs painted with ash-colored dust so that he looked like a figure fashioned from clay, the sight left them gasping in breathless hilarity. But when the boy held aloft what had been revealed before him in the gray barrens, his friends' mirth quieted as they gazed with astonishment at the ring, sunlight caught within the mud-daubed facets of its diamond's sparkling stone.

That object of wonder for the adolescents was an emblem of pain for the young woman who had tossed it into the water eighteen years before, standing at the water's edge in the afternoon glare of a chilly April in 1966, jaw clenched in fury and confusion, not fully knowing she was there at all. In a moment of distraught rage she pulled the engagement ring from her finger and flung it away. The instant it left her hand the woman was stabbed by a terrible regret so acute that she doubled over in a violent soundless sob before the ring had even plunked through the surface, wanting back that small inanimate scrap of the man she loved, the fiancé she'd caught with the sister of her best friend, fleeing what she had witnessed to drive the town's roads without purpose until arriving at the reservoir.

She will have been married to another man for over a decade the year the reservoir is drained, her dull white gold wedding ring a reminder of the infidelity that had so desolated her, tingeing her marriage with an everpresent shade of bitterness. But the woman will take delight in her two children if not in her

13

spouse, the boy thirteen and the girl eleven when she reads about the sturgeon in the county paper, recalling the panicked desperation that had caused her to splash headlong into the cold water in the hope she might somehow recover what she had thrown into it, the flame orange skirt she'd worn buoying up around her like a blooming poppy.

In time the lake will refill by rains and the inexhaustible groundspring that feeds the creek it has always sustained: an unending flow carved between the great folds of hills and ridges above whose peaks the high rocking drift of vultures speck the sky. Steelhead and smelt make their home in the creek's current, just as the giant sturgeon once did as a minuscule fry no bigger than a penny, hatched before the reservoir's dam was built until one day finding its way into the lake to grow larger than any of those born of the cluster of eggs from which it had emerged.

The creek nourishes laurel and willow and manzanita and the ubiquitous black oaks of this region of the world, moss draped and stolid and under whose branches deer step to dip their heads at the bank and drink, ears tipped alert toward any whisper of menace. It wends its way on a southeasterly route, in places surging around lichen-covered rocks, in places falling in stepped white cascades over stone shelves and promontories hidden by curtains of fern. In winter the rains that come in from the Pacific and turn the dry hills' bright flaxen grasses emerald also swell the creek: a rapid rush running through the narrow fog-shrouded valleys of those hills. By early summer the roaring creek becomes a gentle ribbon that meanders slowly toward the bay, the season when ropy clutches of toads' eggs hatch into schools of tadpoles in the creek's pools, their dark brown bodies glinting sparse flecks of yellow as though sprinkled with gold dust held fast by the glossy slime of their skin.

These are what the boys sought to capture on a July afternoon in 1980. Donny Hogg round and heavyset, Aaron Holiman whippet thin, the two carefully picking their way through blackberry brambles to slide down the creek's steep root-laced banks four miles from its origin. They came to hunt tadpoles with a goldfish net and Tupperware container where the creek runs between a shopping center and the town's public library, an arched wooden bridge spanning the water to complete a footpath through a seldom used park. The boys came to the same spot just as they had on many other afternoons this summer between the fifth and sixth grades, intending to add to the toad larvae already growing in a kiddie pool in Aaron's backyard. Now they stood beside the placid water of an inlet pool, looking toward the ground and the child there at their feet.

It was small and skinny and naked but for a roiling swaddle of ants, head covered with a tattered plastic bag. It lay curled against a tree root, wine-dark and rigid and dusted with earth like a root itself.

Donny brushed at the nape of his neck where a mosquito lingered. Aaron opened his mouth as though to speak but then closed it again in an attempt to maintain a silence he sensed ought not to be breached, nervously fingering the straps of the frayed little backpack he wore. The water's soft burble seemed to grow louder in his ears, an otherwise gentle background sound now inexorable.

Aaron crooked his head to look away from what he and Donny stared at in transfixed engrossment but his eyes would not unfasten themselves. He chewed his lip, bothered now by the reason they had come in the first place. For more than the acquisition of fresh tadpoles to replace those that had died or been eaten by nighttime raccoons, the pair had come with greater eagerness to look again at the magazine.

It had been pilfered from a collection Donny's father stored on a hidden bookshelf in an alcove of his garage, a place the boys found behind a wheeled tool cart rolled aside to retrieve the basketball that had hurtled away from them and careened inside the open garage door. There in the cool musty air they'd flipped furtively and excitedly through dozens of pages, lifting their heads every so often in restless anxiety at the possibility of being caught. In order to study the pictures that held them mesmerized they had taken a two-year-old issue of *Oui*, making sure all was back in its place before riding away on their bicycles, adrenalin in their blood. At the creek they pored over the magazine's electrifying photographs, bickering over whose turn it was to hold glossy pages where women in soft focus touched their tongues to crimson lips, red-nailed fingertips resting on what lay between their legs. And the most spellbinding photos: those of women and men doing what the boys had only vaguely imagined by way of rumors and jokes and the roundabout explanations of parents on how babies came into the world. When they were done they wrapped the magazine in a shred of black plastic torn from the liner of one of the park's trash cans and buried it in the creekbed's sandy soil, a shard of old terra cotta drainage pipe washed downstream placed atop the illicit grave mound to mark the spot.

"Why d'you think they killed it?" Donny said.

Aaron looked at his friend and then set his gaze back where Donny's eyes had not moved. The gravity of their discovery trickled through him, proof of some great truth he wished not to be true. "I don't know," he mumbled. He shrugged the nylon backpack from his shoulders and let it drop. The tadpole-catching equipment inside rattled, disquieting the water skimmers resting on the inlet's surface tension so that they skittered away, small ripples unsettling what was mirrored there. "Maybe it didn't get killed," he said halfheartedly. "Maybe it got lost by somebody. Got lost and fell down here."

Donny gave Aaron a dubious glance. "What about that bag, though?" he said, looking back down at the child.

The boys fell into silence again, watching the small cadaver with the scores and scratches in its flesh as though it might offer up some solution as to its life or lack thereof. The clear plastic produce bag over its head was ragged with slits and puncture holes, secured around the child's impossibly slim neck with a thick rubber band like those used to bind ribs of grocery store celery. Any hint of a visage that might be visible was obscured by the spatter of earth covering it, ants scuttling over the hills and valleys of its drooped creases.

An earth-caked length of scabby umbilical cord obtruded from the infant's stomach, the dense horde of ants boiling around it like the nucleus of a small dark galaxy. A lone yellowjacket harassed a large cut on one of the child's twig-thin legs, its own threadlike wasp's legs dangling mid-air where it hovered at the burgundy wound like a hummingbird at a fuchsia blossom.

"Roshambo to see who has to touch it," Donny said, putting forth a pudgy fist. Aaron slapped it away, revolted by the gesture's crassness. "You're sick."

"Just c'mon."

"No way."

"Loser touches it, winner goes and tells somebody."

"I'm not gonna touch it," Aaron said. "We can both go tell, anyway."

"What if the killer comes back to get it?"

"That's bull." Aaron watched the yellowjacket land on the child's leg, its sectioned black-and-yellow body brightly vivid against the gash it crawled atop.

"Or what if a dog gets it?" Donny said. "Or vultures, maybe."

"You're full of it."

"Never know, man. Somebody should stay."

Aaron frowned in deliberation. He thought of the afternoon his father had picked him up from a birthday party on the outskirts of town when he was in third grade, driving along a rural stretch of avenue that ran between horse farms and cow pastures. The car had swerved suddenly, his father maneuvering to avoid a vulture sitting inexplicably in the middle of the road. "Judas priest!" his father had exclaimed, blowing a breath of relief as he straightened out the car. "Thought that thing was a bike tire. Why in hell's it on the road like that?" Aaron had unbuckled his seatbelt and scrambled up in the passenger seat to look through the rear window at the receding creature. The huge bird was strangely calm where it rested on the yellow dividing line, its ugly bald red head hunched atop a body of black feathers, peering after the car with an eerie tranquility. Aaron was astonished at how large the vulture was: a sharp close-up of those he'd seen coasting high above the ridge behind his house in slow circumnavigation. When he was small his mother told him the distant halo meant that something had died below where they circled, that they were waiting to eat as all things must, that they were made to eat what had already passed away. But the boy had also seen the birds on television and now thought of those images from *Wild Kingdom*: the scavengers' grotesque featherless heads disappearing into the rib cages of what remained of wildebeests and zebras, emerging blood-stained and yanking at the sinewy remains they fought over, hissing like cats.

Aaron turned his head up toward the weave of tree limbs above, rays of sunlight through the interlinked branches in a dense pattern of daytime stars. He put his eyes back on the baby, kicking out the toe of his sneaker to shoo away the yellowjacket. "No do-overs," he said quietly. "No two's out of three's."

They shook their fists three times and thrust their hands toward each other simultaneously to throw rock-paper-scissors. Aaron held his hand out flat. Donny showed two fingers and nodded silently at his victory, without the taunting fanfare he might have otherwise exclaimed at scissors trumping his friend's paper.

Aaron pulled his hand back, massaging it as though it had fallen asleep. He shuffled nervously in place, brittle oak leaves and eucalyptus blades crackling beneath his sneakers like desiccated parchment sheaves gone to pieces. He regarded this contract as one that went beyond pacts that were normally decided so, covenants furiously held to since the boys had befriended each other in third grade by virtue of the fact that their surnames each began with H, their desks assigned alphabetically by the pallid skeleton of a teacher who wielded her cane like a sword, fating her pupils to their spots.

Aaron looked at Donny with an expression of grave unease and then crouched down on the sloping creekbank. He leaned away from the small body even as he reached a hand slowly toward it. The reflection of his arm appeared in the inlet's still water, the tip of his cautious forefinger on the tip of the infant's own miniscule finger. He straightened back up with a startled jump, frightened by the lifelessness of what he'd hardly touched. The summer air was warm and the little finger had not been cold. But it did not radiate its own warmth, something it had not done since first emerging into the world thirteen hours earlier, slick and glistening and cradled awkwardly in the hands of the child that had borne it.

The girl had been careful to keep the ever-swelling bump of her belly from her mother, a task made difficult by the fact that she slept on the sofa's fold-out bed in the main room of the small apartment. She hid herself beneath layers of blankets that became hot and unnecessary as the weather grew warmer, hiding what she regarded as an accident like the accident her young mother had on a few occasions told Bitsy she had been, once throwing a heavy glass ashtray that struck the girl in the neck, cigarette butts and gray ash and booze-thickened words falling around her in an angry rain: "You think I had it all planned out? Little baby strollers and all that crap?" Bitsy had said nothing, had not moved to touch her throbbing neck, goosebumps standing up on the girl's flesh like Braille. She'd looked down in order not to meet her mother's livid, inebriated gaze: pinched sour and gargoyle-like and blind with rage.

But her deference did no good, Bitsy's mother lurching forward to yank the lapels of her daughter's yellow terrycloth bathrobe and slap her until Bitsy dropped kneeling to the floor.

The many times Katherine Eddy should have noticed what her daughter tried to conceal she did not, absent from the apartment most afternoons and nights, either at the Laundromat where she worked as an attendant, or in the neighboring town twelve miles north at the house of a man Bitsy knew only as Rex. He was a boyfriend Bitsy's mother said she thought she might marry, another in a long series of boyfriends of whom she'd said similar things, histrionic and smelling of liquor. As Bitsy's breasts and belly grew her mother's carousing no longer pained the girl as it had so many times before, Bitsy relieved by her mother's absence, a non-presence that perdured even when she was home, weaving besotted to the bedroom where she passed out atop the covers, as oblivious as she would have been were she not physically there.

Bitsy made little company with her friends after discovering her pregnancy, companions who grew ever more distant by her repeated refusals to speak about her relationship with the boy Margot and Gwynn were so curious to hear the details of. They called her "stuck-up," calling her more hurtful things as time went on: thinly veiled insults Bitsy endured in silence and which she recalled in bed at night, her mind a hurried hobble of cutting words and cruel altercations and anxieties over the inevitable yet to come. She skipped school more often than she attended and when she did go to classes often arrived after first or second periods or left before the final bell. She wore increasingly baggy clothes and kept to herself, sitting in the school library at a table abutting a window during lunch periods with the pages of open magazines camouflaging books on human anatomy and reproduction, unable to summon up a solution to the dreadful problem that weighted her.

The circuitous route she took home from school sharpened her aloneness. Bitsy walked an extra quarter mile to avoid the Seven-Eleven where she knew Gwynn and Margot would be, where she guessed Art would no longer be to offer her any more rides. Her ride home from the reservoir had been the last time she'd seen him. When they'd arrived at her apartment complex that night she had expected the boy to offer her his telephone number. When he didn't she had asked for it, quietly and with embarrassment. Art had leaned across her impatiently, opening the glove compartment to rummage roughly through a spilling litter of crumpled napkins and candy wrappers and condiment packets, snatching out an old ketchup-stained traffic ticket. He asked her for a pen and she gave him one from her tote bag and he wrote on the back of the citation, numbers childishly large and scrupulous and uneven like those made by a kindergartner only just learning to print. But the many times Bitsy had dialed those distinctively lettered numerals she connected only with a series of tones and a recorded woman's voice, its cold robot's cadence telling her the number had been disconnected or was no longer in service. Art had not gotten out of the running car to open her door for her that night as she expected he would. He had not kissed her goodbye or waved back at her as she waved at him: the boy's tanned arm over the back of the empty passenger seat, his body twisted around toward the rear window to back the Falcon down the steep driveway. The headlights washed her white-skinned and featureless until the car turned and the lights vanished and the girl stood alone in darkness, surrounded by the rhythmic thrum of cricketsong.

When the school year ended Bitsy spent her solitary days watching television, the closed blinds and curtains rimmed by the light of early summer sun, the tiny apartment becoming a dark, lonesome womb lit only by the flicker of game shows and soap operas. Occasionally the girl left her gloomy sanctuary to wander up Grant Avenue, buying crackers and SpaghettiOs and packages of red licorice from a liquor store on the corner of First Street with the few dollar bills and stacks of Laundromat quarters her mother left for her on the kitchen table. Sometimes she bought a Coke from the ancient machine inside the fire station across the street, brief respite from her hours of seclusion.

She'd first wandered past the fire station on an afternoon in early June, a group of firemen sitting on folding lawn chairs at the mouth of the station's open garage, lounging and joking and sipping from shapely bottles of Coca-Cola. Bitsy only ever saw Coke in cans or plastic two-liter bottles but remembered the glass bottles from when she was little. One of the firemen saw her pause to regard his drink and made a beckoning gesture, reaching into his pocket to retrieve a dime. He held it out in the middle of his large palm where it winked small and silver in the sunlight. Though Bitsy had learned to hide herself well, she knew that he and the other men noticed the lump beneath the overly large blue shift she wore, her milk-heavy breasts. But if they recognized her condition they made no mention of it either by word or expression and so she had come forward shyly at the firefighter's urging nod, snatching up the coin like a wary bird. The T-shirted fireman had smiled, motioning with his thumb to the garage behind him. Bitsy hesitated, then walked into the cool garage where a tall red fire engine and a paramedic rescue truck sat parked, making her way through that narrow canyon between them to the back of the garage where an old-fashioned Coke machine sat. Its once red paint had faded to a rosy pink, the patina of rust at the steel edges of its slender glass door so perfectly ordinary it seemed as though the corrosion had been intentionally worked into the metal; or had emerged by some innate natural design the way a newly budded leaf contains the thing that will in time cause it to redden and dry and fall from its limb. She'd stood admiring the antiquated vending machine, dropping the dime flatways into the wide slot and opening the cooler door to pull out one of the bottles by its neck, delighted by the aged mechanism's inexplicable graciousness.

She came to the station regularly afterwards, the firemen always friendly even when shifts had changed and they were men she did not recognize, never objecting when she walked uninvited into the garage. "Hey there, Sodapop" one had begun saying.

The others began saying the same thing when they saw her, Bitsy nodding and grinning tight-lipped and saying "Hey" back in a quiet voice, hurrying toward the machine she had come to love for its modest constancy. The visits became a ritual: placing a dime in the slot and opening the door and retrieving a bottle and levering its top against the built-in opener, the bottlecap dropping down to disappear into some mysterious receptacle with a thin clink. And then the girl would linger there in the cool quiet beside the machine's faint hum, savoring the serenity of that soft unvarying drone.

When Bitsy stepped back out into the sun she never stayed long enough to converse with the firemen about anything more than how hot it was and how good it was to have a cold Coke, telling them she had to go. She knew the bottles were re-used and on return visits sometimes brought a few back, placing them into the spaces of plastic crates stacked beside the machine. But most she saved; the thick bottles rinsed-out and set next to another, their clear aquamarine glass the color of swimming pool water. "Hey there," Bitsy would say, setting down the most recently acquired next to the others, "Hey there, Sodapop," arranging them like a collection of cherished dolls in a row on the apartment's tiny concrete balcony.

She was on the balcony the night it was time.

It was a Friday evening, her mother with Rex for the weekend. Bitsy lay on the sofa in a thin summer nightgown, the television on but the girl paying little attention to the show on the screen, its images and voices mere company. She stirred her spoon in what muddled milk remained in a bowl of Life cereal balanced precariously atop the ledge of fabric stretched taut between her knees.

She got up and carried the bowl to the small kitchen, setting it down in the sink. Bitsy opened the sliding glass door and stepped out into the warm July night, the air flavored with the sharp resinous scent from the upper branches of a tall pine that abutted the second storey balcony, its sprawl of unpruned limbs poking over and through the low railing. The tree was strung with fat Christmas lights never removed by whoever had put them up: bulging colored bulbs that sat unlit and forgotten within a dense mass of bristling needles.

Bitsy turned toward her arrangement of empty Coke bottles, admiring their elegantly curved shapes by the light that came through the door. The insides of her thighs warmed and her feet wetted and she looked down: a wet shine in the yellow light. For a moment the girl stood uncomprehending, thinking she had somehow peed herself. But then her heart leaped into her throat with the realization of what was happening and she hurried back into the kitchen, petrified, trying to remember what to do. She grabbed the handle of a bread knife from its wooden block holder on the counter and stumbled in a rush toward the bathroom.

She stripped off her soaked underpants and lay down in the bathtub, a seep of water still coming from her. For a time there was nothing, none of the things she'd read would happen. The windowless little bathroom was stuffy by the summer heat, Bitsy's face already flushed and shining with perspiration when she felt a fullness in her abdomen: an overstuffed pinch like a gas bubble. The pinch became a cramp and then another and then a series of cramps, coming in waves that grew more frequent, more intense. She breathed hard, panting breaths hitched and gasping, wishing there was someone beside her, Gwynn or Margot, even Art. She pictured his hand atop hers where it gripped the side of the tub, the mustachioed boy stroking her damp forehead. But in the midst of a cramp that seized her so viciously she ground her teeth, Bitsy felt suddenly stupid for thinking such a thing, for having harbored any hope toward him. Though she'd noticed every white car that passed her on the street, following them with her eyes in anticipation of catching sight of his, she had not seen the boy once in the months since they'd been together at the reservoir, remembering the coldness he'd showed her on the drive home, the many calls she'd made to a made-up phone number.

Bitsy struggled up to her knees, pulling on the plastic shower curtain for support until it snapped from two of the rings on the rod above. Her diaphanous cotton nightgown had become drenched through with sweat, the thin fabric sticking translucently to the teenager like a constricting second skin she wriggled to be free of. She grunted and yelped; sometimes so loudly she worried the sounds she could not keep herself from barking might be heard through the walls by a neighbor.

For three hours the pains in her abdomen swelled and ebbed and then returned again until the girl felt a great charge go through her. She sat up, pressing her back against the bathtub's porcelain to brace herself into a kind of squat, feeling a great need to push and pushing, mouth open, eyes squinched tightly shut by the intolerable hurt. When she opened them she saw it. So small between her knees: gray and grimace-faced and slicked with blood.

In his recoiling leap away from the child Aaron's foot slid on the soft earth and into the water with a mild sploosh. He stood in a wide straddle: one foot on dry ground, the other in the inlet pool. Donny tried to stifle a laugh while Aaron contorted his wiry physique so that his other foot would not slip too, leaping from the pond with a nimble hop. He stepped angrily toward Donny, jabbing his friend hard in the side. "Dickhead."

Donny crimped sideways, stepping away, "What's your problem?"

"Why're you laughing?"

"I didn't mean anything."

"How come I had to touch it, anyway?"

"You lost."

Aaron plopped down and took off his wet sneaker and tilted it, a trail of water draining out over the ground. "How come we had to mess around with it in the first place?" he said.

"Don't be so pissed, man. I'll touch it too."

Aaron stood up. He shoved his friend but his thin frame only caused Donny's solid weight to falter slightly in place. "You better goddam not," he said. Aaron sat back down and stripped off his wet sock, now dirt-covered and spangled with leaves. "Go tell somebody."

"You can go," Donny said. "I don't care."

"I'm staying here."

"No big deal, I can stay."

"No way," Aaron said, shaking his head. He unlaced his sneaker and put it on his bare foot, retying it. "No way," he said again as he stood up, afraid Donny would harass the little body were he to be left alone with it: poking the child with a stick the way he did the carcasses of car-killed skunks and raccoons and opossums they sometimes found along roadsides, prodding and stirring at their remains as though trying to divine something from the drying entrails. Aaron pointed a finger at his friend, "You're going."

"We both can go."

"That's what I said before we did roshambo, retard," Aaron said. He tossed his dirty white tube sock at Donny. It missed, landing on a sunlit tuft of sedgegrass. "I'm staying, you're going."

Donny put up his hands, "Alright. Okay."

Aaron stayed where he was while Donny began climbing the steep bank, slipping as he clambered up through the brush, loose rocks and dirt clods rolling down behind him. Aaron shifted himself to shield the baby from being struck by the miniature landslide made by his companion's clumsy efforts. Even in Aaron's unrest at their discovery and his exasperation with Donny's irreverent attitude, he felt a twinge of pity for his friend: a fat kid forced to endure taunts and teases at school because of his weight and unfortunate surname, coping with the constant cruelty by displaying a churlish bravado that Aaron found funny. Aaron did not find his friend's glib bluster funny now, watching Donny Hogg's flabby form grasp at exposed tree roots in his graceless struggle up the creekbank until he reached the top of the embankment and disappeared.

Aaron turned toward the child and squatted down. The plastic bag covering its head seemed more forbidding now that he was alone with the tiny body. But he duck-walked cautiously nearer the infant until he was beside it, his eleven-year-old curiosity prevailing over his fear. He leaned his small face closer and saw that the bevy of ants crawling over the child was composed of an elaborate series of trails: bits of flesh and dried umbilical cord carried away to some subterranean nest. Spots of water rested on the skinny newborn's small swollen belly like translucent pearls, a spare constellation of liquid beads that had splashed from Aaron's slip into the pool. He blew on one to break its surface tension and watched the waterbead lose its shape and run in a streak down the child's side, carrying away the dust and ants in its path, a portion of slash wound washed the color of ruby.

Aaron eased out of his crouch and sat, looking at the pond where his reflection and that of the baby hovered over a small school of tadpoles. They swam blackly like squiggling commas, congregating in rows at the pool's shallow edges to feed on the fuzz of algae there. In the astonishment of their encounter the boys had failed to notice them and Aaron felt a pang of shame, knowing that had he and Donny not discovered the child they still would not have used the net and plastic tub in his backpack, that they would have spent the afternoon sitting at the water's edge looking at the dug-up magazine. The magazine will not be disinterred again. Moisture will eventually seep through the makeshift plastic casing the boys had wrapped it in, warping and fusing the pages together into a disintegrating lump of pulp. The creek will eventually swell by winter rains, covering over the magazine's resting place until the wet glop of pages are carried away altogether, preserved only by Aaron Holiman's memory of it, the thing he and his friend had come to look at that day and what they had inadvertently found.

Aaron looked again at the baby next to him, considering the stripe the water bead had left in its wake: a clean thin part through dirt and ants. Although he knew that like vultures the ants only did what they were made to, the slow devouring disturbed him. He glanced at the sock he had tossed at Donny. It hung in a heavy wet droop, soil-smudged and crumpled like something fallen from a laundry hamper. Aaron pondered using it to wipe the ants off. But he left the sock where it lay, not wanting to touch the infant again, knowing that even with something between his hand and the tiny corpse he would still be aware of its heatlessness. Dirtier than a dirty sock, he thought, a thing he'd worn on his foot. And so he stood and went to his backpack and zipped it open and took out the round white Tupperware tub, returning to the infant with the container and removing the lid, dipping the opaque plastic bowl into the pool to fill it.

Creekwater poured from the plastic container in a wide flat cascade, bouncing off the dirt and insects that covered the infant in a splashing spatter. Aaron chewed at his lip, dissatisfied. He refilled the Tupperware bowl and emptied it over the baby once more, pouring slower this time, more carefully, the cake of earth beginning to come away in muddy rivulets, bits of leaf and thorny twig and wriggling clumps of ants carried off by the tiny flood. Aaron filled the bowl a third time, dousing the child to wash away what still clung to it until its body was fully exposed: stiff-limbed and beet purple, mapped with a latticework of scrapes and scratches that caused the boy to stand and take a step away, awestruck by the brutality the wounds disclosed. The afternoon sun had shifted, shining through the canopy of trees over the creekbed so that the boy and the skinny newborn were striped in bands of gold and shadow. Aaron had tried to avoid getting the plastic bag wet but it was now sodden and wilted, the infant's tiny face showing through in membranous relief: a nose, eyelids, the thin line of its lips frozen open like the mouth of a fish.

Bitsy crimped over to lift the child, its body so small and slight it made her own small hands seem like a giant's brawny paws. She regarded the baby for a long moment, stunned at the paradoxical marvel of what had come from her: a helpless, feeble thing writhing with life in the gory attire of something slain.

She pulled away the sticky mucous that covered it and leaned back to place the child on her chest and picked up the serrated bread knife she'd set by the side of the tub. The girl severed the hot cable that connected her to the infant's belly, holding the slippery spiral of cord in the air. She remembered that she was supposed to have clamped it off beforehand and with her other arm leaned over the bathtub and threw open the cupboard beneath the sink, rummaging blindly for something she could use to tie it with, knocking over unseen items until her

43

palm closed around a dental floss dispenser. The baby began squirming atop her. Then it began to wail: a noise high and shrill and halting. In the midst of the child's squalls Bitsy worked to loop the maddeningly fine thread around and around the coil of flesh she held, struggling with it as though wrestling to subdue a serpent.

Bitsy pushed herself up in a numb of pain, the baby tucked awkwardly into the crook of her arm. She stepped from the tub and faltered to the bathroom's towel cupboard, shoving over bottles of lotions and astringents and a dish of seashell-shaped soaps arranged atop its mildewed yellow paint. She set the newborn down in their place and stood looking at it like someone drugged or somnambulant, bloodshot eyes on the infant's glistening nakedness. Its small hands were curled into fists, skinny legs punching jerkily at the air. The shoddily tied length of whorled cord hanging from the infant's belly shivered with each of its froglike kicks, kicks Bitsy had felt in her belly during the months she had carried it. The other half dangled from her like a stray intestine. Bitsy knew from the books she'd clandestinely researched at school that afterbirth would come. But she didn't know what to do until it did, anxious over the wavering bawls the angry red newborn cuffed into the airless bathroom, each preceded by a brief pause, the child drawing in breaths that exploded from its scrunched face in furious squeals that echoed against the tiled walls.

She set about tying two towels together to secure between her legs, frustrated when the bulky diaper fell apart, trying again clumsily to fashion something to staunch the blood and water that issued from her. While she fumbled with the towels blood darker than any she had ever seen poured from her, then a heap of gray-blue viscera that slid down the insides of her thighs and onto the linoleum like organs spilling from something disemboweled. Bitsy stooped to gather up the large unwieldy mess that lay between her feet with a fatigued relief that overrode the horror she might otherwise have felt. She plopped the mass of gore into the bathtub, taken aback by how big it was, how it covered over the drain in a tangled mound.

The girl was now so streaked with blood and sweat it was as though she herself had just been born, hair matted to her head and neck like a glossy bonnet of feathers. She pulled the saturated nightgown up over the top of her head and let it drop, standing unclothed and exhausted, bewildered. The bathroom was wet and blood-pink and disarranged, tile cleansers and Q-tips and old medicine bottles spilled onto the floor from the sink cabinet where she'd grabbed the dental floss. A box of cotton balls lay tipped-over, those that had rolled from its open top lying on the linoleum fat and miserable-looking by the moisture they'd absorbed. In years to come the persistent hauntings that visited Bitsy would carry with them not an image of the baby, but that of the disheveled bathroom and the blurred reflection of herself in the fog-edged mirror: a still life of the place she'd stood frightened and naked and alone in the quiet.

The quiet.

In her post-partum fugue Bitsy had not noticed that the pauses between the baby's cries had begun to lengthen, its high-pitched howls growing ever fainter until the wailing stopped altogether. When she did discern the silence she turned back to the top of the cupboard to see that the child's tiny gum-rimmed mouth had taken on a weirdly misshapen aspect, the expression on its small face inscrutable: one of decrepitude and elderliness and something Bitsy did not recognize for never having seen it.

Her eyes widened with the realization that what had come from her living now no longer breathed. But when Bitsy put a hand above its little nose and mouth found that the child did yet live, though scarcely, the breaths she felt on her palm so shallow as to be almost imperceptible. She hurriedly wrapped the infant in a worn yellow hand towel. To keep it warm, she told herself, knowing that the terrycloth she'd completely cloaked the child in might hinder the paltry lungfuls of air it was still able to muster.

Bitsy picked up the newborn and fled the bathroom. She knelt naked on the floor and dumped out her tote bag and placed the towel-swathed child at the bottom and put back what she had removed: a spiral notebook and binders and a thick civics textbook she had never opened or returned to the first period class she'd missed nearly the entire spring semester, placing everything atop the newborn in terrified concealment; in the guilty knowledge of what she did.

She returned to the bathroom and washed herself of sweat and bloodstains as best she could and then went to the small dresser beside the sofa, putting on a pair of underpants she stuffed with T-shirts and tank tops. She wiggled into her loose blue shift and jogged to the kitchen, pausing long enough to fill a glass of water at the sink. Bitsy drank from it in rough gulps and refilled it to drink again, water spilling down over the mounds of her swollen breasts. She went back to the sofa and put on her sneakers and took up the tote, hurrying out the apartment door with the canvas bag slung over her shoulder like a purse.

In the girl's stupefied journey in those hours after midnight the dribble of bloody water would not stop despite the improvised padding she wore, the bulk of T-shirts between her legs turning her stride into an ungainly waddle. She walked over a mile with the towel-bound child at the bottom of the tote bag, not knowing where it was she went or what assistance she might find when she arrived. Who would help her? She muttered a prayer, wondering if it was even a prayer at all. Or if it was heard, unsure in what regard she was held in the eyes of what she was equally unsure was. "Please" was all she could think to assemble. She repeated the simple appeal in a whisper so soft and irresolute the word barely left her chapped lips. Wet sneaker prints followed her, gleaming under streetlamps' lights like puddles of new rainwater.

Thumping footsteps carried over the water from the bridge upstream, voices. Aaron straightened and went to the creekshore and pushed aside a branch and saw Donny leading an older boy wearing a red apron to the middle of the bridge. Donny gestured up at the teenage boy, pointing and waving, guiding the teen back off the bridge the way they had come. Aaron stayed where he was at the water's edge as Donny's chattering voice came nearer, eyes unfocused on the shore opposite, listening to the small sound of rushing water where it ran through the upturned shopping cart. A blackbird alighted on the cart's rusting steel basket, jerking its head one way and then another, a tiny golden eye tilted toward the creek. The bird looked toward him with one fleet movement as though he were a curiosity to be mildly vigilant of. And then it made a short *quip!* and took flight, darting weightlessly upward into the trees.

Brush rustled and crunched behind him and Aaron turned to see Donny sliding down the embankment, a thick length of blackberry vine sticking to his shirt like something determined to prevent his descent. "Damnit!" Donny cursed. He landed in the flat creekbed with a stumbling roll and stood up brushing at his clothes, face and neck and arms specked with dirt stuck to the sheen of sweat on his skin. He looked at the newly rinsed-off child, its nakedness starker and unequivocal. "Oh," he said softly.

A voice came from the top of the creekbank: "I can't get down there, kid."

Donny turned and cupped his hands around his mouth, "It's right here!"

The brush crackled again as the aproned teen came slowly down, a boy with long blonde hair and acne-blighted skin. Donny had spotted him along the footpath between the shopping center and the park, the teen whistling blithely as he pushed a clattering train of stray shopping carts back toward the supermarket, Donny hollering after him until the older boy stopped and turned, half-listening to what the grade-schooler excitedly told him, a jaded expression on his blemished face. "You Doug Spear's little brother?" he'd interrupted. "Spear put you up to this?" He looked over Donny's head toward the park, scanning it through squinted eyes. "Somewhere down there smoking a joint, probably." But when Donny let out an exasperated sigh and turned to jog off in search of someone else, the teenager relented. "Alright, show me," he'd said, scooting the interlocked line of carts off the path. "Spear's down there, right? Him and Romano?"

Now the teen tussled with blackberry thorns that caught and pulled at his clothes, his hands behind him on the steep bank's loose earth as he made short little steps to keep from falling. Once in the creekbed he blew out a breath and began fiddling with his red apron, preoccupied with a long ragged tear made by a thorn still stuck in the fabric.

"Look man," Donny said impatiently. "Man, look!"

The acne-faced boy raised his head, arching an eyebrow in smug nonchalance as he stepped toward where Donny pointed. "Spear?" he said, swiveling his head as though expecting an ambush. But then the teenager's bemused expression melted. He saw what lie on the ground blood-scored and shining wetly in the rain of light from the trees, his acned face candid and unselfconscious as he bowed his skinny frame over the child. "Holy…" he said quietly, what words might have followed trailing away.

Bitsy arrived at the shopping center in the pre-dawn hours, worn-out and wobbly, toddling through the large empty parking lot where skinny lightpoles cast ocher circles over the blacktop. She walked through the artificial pools of light, over countless white lines that in daylight would have cars and trucks parked between them in ordered rows, now devoid of the meaning those painted stripes were meant to demarcate. The night was still and silent, Bisty trekking on through the fearsome summer calm not knowing where it was she went or what she would do when she arrived, fleeing from what lay at the bottom of the tote bag she carried. She travelled the wide concrete walkway along the shopping center's storefronts, past the half-darkened windows of Long's Drugs and Great Western Savings, their deserted interiors cast in dusky gloom by the few fluorescent lights that remained on inside: counters and checkout lanes cold and remote even in their closeness. She turned a corner past the closed wooden shutters of a florist's stand and stopped, taking the tote from her shoulder to rest beside a small bakery. The shop exuded the faint sweet scent of bread, dark inside but for a warm yellow light under the display counter. Stacked chairs and wrought iron tables brought in for the night crowded the shop's interior, the display case light shining through their curved shapes and shadows in intricate designs that looped and coiled one within another in a multivalent labyrinth that seemed to possess neither beginning nor end.

Bitsy stood near the light, shadows tattooed across her face. She wanted to stay where she was in that small peaceful place but knew she couldn't and so dropped her head and took up the tote and ambled on, stepping from the dimly lit walkway onto a narrow path that led to the park near the rear of the shopping center. The moon was new and the sky cast no illumination but for a smatter of stars, the walkway's tawny lamps fading behind her as she went. Bitsy knew the path would lead her to the bridge that spanned the creek, but she did not know where it was she travelled any more than she did when she'd first left the apartment.

Chittering screeches came from the dark ahead, sharp and feral. The girl stopped and looked back toward the lights she had left. She knew the sounds were only raccoons bickering with one another, vicious gabbling noises she occasionally heard from the apartment's balcony, sometimes accompanied by the thunderous metallic racket of a garbage can being overturned. But her child's mind fashioned them into other things: an amalgam of images cobbled from *Creature Features*, things vampiric and humpbacked and sallow-skinned, their fiends' eyes narrowed with malice. Bitsy watched the show on Saturday nights, lonely and bored in the apartment, unable to resist the television program's horror movies despite the sleeplessness they sometimes gave her. Now the macabre scenes that kept her awake on the fold-out bed suggested themselves anew.

Bitsy veered from the path toward what lights shone from behind the shopping center's storefronts, crashing through a field of summer-dry grass and tall fennel stalks that whipped at her thighs, the diaper of wet T-shirts between her legs coming loose as she tussled through the licorice-scented shoots. But she did not stop, feeling blindly to adjust her panties as she went, wiping her blood-wetted hand on the outside of the tote bag until she emerged from the weed-choked field breathless and straw-speckled, hair diademed with yellow umbels of fennel flower.

She bent to catch her breath on a utility road running parallel the creek. Bitsy straightened and walked in the direction of the light at the rear of the stores, her shadow growing and stretching on the pavement behind her featureless and spectral like an elongated doppelgänger.

A bare fluorescent tube hummed over the big rear doors above a supermarket's loading bay, moths flitting erratic circles around its gum of dust and cobwebs. She went up the curved concrete ramp to the top and eased down beside a stack of plastic milk crates and cardboard boxes. She took the tote's straps from her shoulder and pushed the bag away from her and sat straight-legged with her back against the wall, limbs leaden with fatigue as she massaged her newly flabby abdomen in an attempt to ease the dull ache there. The canvas bag slid easily across concrete slick with the gunk of rotted produce trampled to a vegetal film. The odor of curdled dairy lay in the air, thick and fetid. But the girl was too tired to find a spot less foul-smelling. "Please," she whispered once more, less a word than a faltering sigh of resignation, sincere in its poverty. Something heard, perhaps. Perhaps a mere exhalation of words into indifferent space. The girl didn't know. She looked at the tote. The canvas was burr-covered and marked with the blood-streaks of her fingers; what pending answer she hoped might come by her petition subsumed by what lay beneath the bag's book and binders.

The utility road below lay black and plain and empty in the loading bay's wan light, a place soon to be traversed by forklifts and slow-moving tractor-trailers backing up to deliver their loads as the July sun rose. She stared down at it, startled when a gray cat padded silently into the dirty pool of light. It sensed her and froze, turning its quick head to look up toward where Bitsy sat, the feline's widened eyes throwing back the fluorescence in a green-yellow glow. The cat sprung into the brush in a single mercurial bolt as quickly as it had paused, crouching there amongst trees and weeds and briar bushes that in the bleak light looked like things smudged in charcoal.

Bitsy had had a cat when she was six years old, an orange tabby her mother had given her. She'd named it "Sardine" because that was the first thing Bitsy fed it late one night, picking bits of oily fish from a sardine tin the cat licked from her fingers, laughing at the way its rough little tongue tickled. Her mother had not thought to get cat food. But Katherine Eddy had not thought to get a cat at all, impulsively snatching up a stray after it brushed itself against her leg in the gravel parking lot of a Mexican restaurant where she'd shared pitchers of margaritas with friends one night. The cat had not been a stray but belonged to a family whose house was down the street from the restaurant, the mother and three children spending a week searching the neighborhood and knocking on neighbors' doors asking after it when it didn't return home. And though Bitsy's mother had noticed the cat's white flea collar, she only shrugged off the fact and drove home with the cat mewling in the backseat, swaying into her sleeping daughter's room to wake her and present her with a tom not quite a kitten and not yet a cat, its carrot-colored coat wide-striped and whirled, a series of ginger-hued spots down its white chest like the buttons of a vest. Bitsy played with her new pet constantly, dismayed when it was grabbed by the scruff of its neck by her mother's boyfriend, tossed out the small ramshackle house they'd lived in then, his place, a big, bearded man who went by the nickname Flash and who hated cats and who regularly flung Sardine into the tall unmown grass where tire rims and piles of red bricks and stacks of termite-scourged boards lay overgrown and lichen-spotted. The cat hid from him when the man was home, keeping to the small laundry room at the side of the house where Bitsy sat on an old rag carpet and waggled a piece of springy wire for Sardine to paw and snap at, sometimes bedding a plastic laundry basket with her stuffed animals for him to nap in and one afternoon nodding off there herself, lulled to sleep by the heat and click-clack of the whirring dryer, the steady hiss of winter rain outside the laundry room's sliding glass door. She slept curled beneath a storage shelf low to the floor until she was woken by the hard galumphs of Flash's boots as he came in looking for something on one of the upper shelves, grumbling to himself. Bitsy opened her eyes and through the gaps in the laundry basket saw Sardine hunch down stiffly, his slitted pupils widened black. And when Flash spotted him and reached into the basket Sardine was in the beginnings of a leap away when the big man caught him, sucking air angrily through his teeth as he opened the heavy glass door and threw the cat out. The rain outside turned to a fierce hail the moment the cat landed in the sopping grass. It scrambled back, braving the man's hatred rather than the stinging pellets of ice. But its rocketing trajectory intersected with the closing sliding door before it could slip inside. Bitsy yipped out a cry and scuttled from underneath the shelf on all fours toward her pet where it lay on its side panting tongue-out and scooting around in a slow circle and purring a frightening low-toned growl. Its head had met with the doorjamb, the cat's orange-and-white fur dyed red by what percolated from its ears and eyes. She looked up at her mother's boyfriend from where she knelt on her hands and knees, her face's cast and color and shape transcending her age as though made-up for some silent film: pancaked in ash gray, eyes blackened hollow for a role in which a young girl grows old and becomes a widowed beldam creased by time's loss. She regarded Flash's face as something monstrous and arctic though the rough bearded man's features had become softer than at anytime since his infancy, his mouth agape in guilty disbelief. "We can't let it suffer, babe," He uttered softly. "We can't let it suffer." He knelt down beside Bitsy and told her to leave the laundry room and when she refused, standing to beat him fruitlessly across his wide back with her diminutive fists, he did not insist but bore her howling grief and took the small tom's wet head in his hands and pressed his big thumbs into its throat until it stilled.

Now from where she sat beside the supermarket milk crates she watched the cat's luminous eyes, abiding the uninvited recollection of her own. For memories come unbidden and are permitted right of entry no matter how unwelcome; things neither good nor bad but always both. And so a remembered orange tom with button-down markings on its chest arrives more deeply present in the world for having vanished from it, its mortal throes what preserves the rough tickling of a cat's tongue on a girl's mind's fingers.

Bitsy stared at the reflective disks in the huddled murk of foliage bordering the top of the creekbank until they blinked once and then were gone. She wondered if the cat still spied her from some unseen place, what other eyes might be watching.

The girl looked again at the bulging tote bag beside her, the child in it silent since she'd left home and silent still. She began pulling out the binders and the notebook from the tote, slowly and with reluctance in the knowledge of what she had done. And then the heavy civics textbook, pocked and edgeworn, the image of Mount Rushmore on its cover defaced in thick pencil by whoever had possessed it the school year before: a ghoulish klatch of presidents drawn over with cross-eyes and penis tongues and leering fangs jutting beneath curled moustaches. She set it down, hesitating before getting up on her knees to lift out what she had buried.

It was so light as to be almost weightless. She held the bundle in her hands for only a moment and then laid it down on the rancid concrete and unfolded the discolored towel. The scrawny child was oddly crooked. She saw by the buzzing fluorescent light that its tiny arms and legs had turned pale blue. The tied-off length of umbilical cord lay coiled across the unmoving infant's belly, draped in a fleshy helix like a snake coiled around itself. Bitsy did not want to look at it. But before she could turn away an almost inaudible squeak arrested her in place.

The small sound came again, a slight *cack* like a subtle clearing of the throat. And then a shivering little sigh that trailed away, moving within the baby's chest in that weak act of breathing so that its ribs showed through the child's colorless gray skin as though through paper.

The girl's stone-frozen face slackened into a disbelieving gawp. She ran her hands through her entangled hair and craned her neck forward as though to be sure that it had woken, horror-struck at the possibility that its toothless little mouth might open wider to recommence its terrible wailing.

Bitsy looked around frantically, scuttling along on

her knees amongst the debris of cardboard scraps and wire ties and rubber bands and plastic container lids scattered over the liquefying vegetable mush. She found a clear plastic produce bag and picked it up and held it bunched in her palm and turned back to the child, watching its fragile breathing, the insubstantial piece of plastic weighing heavy in her hand.

But then she bent forward, swiftly and with her eyes shut tight against what she did. She hooded the motionless infant by touch alone and then let go and snatched up a fat rubber band, unwilling to hold the bag in place herself. She stretched the band out with both hands, forced to look to see where it was to be put, slipping it over the child's bag-covered head gently and gingerly as though afraid to hurt it, down around its thin neck as though it were the collar of a sweater. When she let go a short sharp snap echoed briefly against the supermarket wall.

The bag sagged like a half-deflated balloon with the air that had become trapped inside it, enormous around the baby's tiny head. Bitsy's breath caught fast in her lungs and she held it there, heartbeat pumping in her ears. The child began to move: slow and sluggish, its tiny blue fists quaking uselessly at its sides, stick legs pedaling feebly at the air as though in a leaden jog through the landscape of some dream or nightmare.

The girl released her breath. "Oh my God."

Bitsy scooted away and vomited over the edge of the loading bay. She retched once again and then lay down panting, curled-up with an arm beneath her head, the bitter taste of bile in her mouth. A frog began croaking from somewhere down the creekbank. The amphibian's throaty chirp was joined by another and then another and then still more: their rachety chorus growing and layering and amplifying upon itself; what might have been something striking in its natural beauty to Bitsy's ears nothing better than ugly dissonance.

She crawled back toward the crates and boxes and knelt once more beside the baby. It had ceased moving, a portion of the bag drawn against the newborn's delicate features in a creased membrane where its small open mouth had sought air. Bitsy fought back renewed nausea as she shrouded the child in the towel it laid on, putting the binders and notebook and textbook back in the tote bag, this time with the child atop them. Then she waggled hastily down the loading bay ramp, one hand dragging the tote bag, the other pulling on the elastic of her underpants to shore up the crude padding of T-shirts there.

Bitsy walked the utility road the way she had come, the frogs' raucous choir a rasping blare like the riotous heckling of a stadium's crowd whose censorious roar she was the object of. Even as she stumbled back through the field of weeds to the park's path she could hear them. She rushed on past the path and past the arched wooden bridge, the oaks and thick blackberry canes lining the top of the creekbank shapes only just visible by the distant lights of the shopping center.

The vague edges of a bench formed itself from the dimness. The girl stopped. She set the tote bag atop the bench and sat, no longer afraid of what things she'd earlier imagined the dark might contain. She slouched and closed her eyes, inhaling the fresh stony scent of water drifting up from the creek below, half-wishing for the unending sleep of the life that had come from her hours earlier. And then Bitsy did fall asleep, suddenly and heavily with her chin dropped to her chest: a dozing figure unknown and unseen and alone beside the creek's unceasing, twitching in a dream of lightlessness so black it woke her again.

The girl sat bolt upright, eyes open from dark to dark. For a moment she was confused by the nothingness she had dreamt, by the blankness that surrounded her in her waking. She shifted on the bench, listening now for the frogs' sounds as some proof of where she was. But there was only the sound of the creek. The girl wondered over the difference between putting from sight what she had kept from sight all the months she carried the child and carried still. Was it a thing if only she knew it was? Bitsy shook her head of the inscrutable puzzle, pushing the tips of her fingers at the edges of her eyes as she tilted her head back.

Stars peeked from between the gnarled shadows of oak branches above her. She recalled the sky the evening she'd been with Art at the reservoir, how he'd put his arm around her and caressed the back of her neck and whispered in her ear and then took her chin in his hand, turning it to his face, kissing her. They'd kissed and kissed and she'd tasted his tongue in her mouth and soon his hands were on her breasts. And then Art had hopped from the picnic table and led her by the hand, lying down in the grass and motioning for her to lie beside him. The newly darkened sky had been a deep blue-black, the light from a bright newly risen moon overpowering the light of what stars might be seen. He had been gentle at first, touching her lightly as he slid her underpants from beneath her skirt, kneeling up to undo the belt of his jeans and kicking off the cowboy boots he wore. But then he had been rough, heavy atop her so that she could barely breathe, buried within the tall blades of grass that surrounded her so that all she could see was the boy's jerking silhouette, the round white moon behind him. It had been coarse and forceful and hurt the way she'd heard it might hurt. But it had been quick and she'd made no complaint nor put up any resistance, proud to no longer be a childish virgin like Margot or Gwynn or any of the other freshman girls who pretended to know what she could now claim. When the boy was done he'd lain limply atop her, a weighty shadow panting stale breath against her face.

She thought of what had come of those few minutes in the grass: of what she had carried and undergone and how she had wished and waited for time to hasten and how it had only crept along. She thought of an afternoon when she sat alone in the apartment's kitchen and watched the thin red second hand swoop around the dial of the brass and enamel wall clock. It had occurred to Bitsy that its movement was as meaningless as the minute and hour hands or the clock's curlicued numbers, how one might as well tell time by watching a dog chase its tail; that minutes and hours were as made-up as anything else that could be invented. The thought had vexed her and she'd put it from her mind. But now the idea returned with greater potency, the girl uncertain whether there were any endings at all. She had waited and worried and now that the waiting was over it seemed things had only commenced anew and with a greater weightiness.

There in the blackness where she sat on a park bench the girl wished for someone to be with her, thinking despite herself of Art and his tenderness at the picnic table by the reservoir and longing now for some affection akin to it: some simple embrace or gentle hairline stroke. She did not know and would never know that earlier that night while she lay spraddle-legged and groaning in a bathtub, Arthur Dolcini lay in a small cemetery two miles away.

"Horny cooze," he'd slurred, the orange tip of the cigarette in his mouth bouncing in the moonless dark as he spoke, bragging about a girl he claimed to have had sex with there in the town's oldest cemetery. Art sat reclined against a headstone illuminated by an upended flashlight beside him, the three friends to whom he boasted soon to begin their last year at the high school he no longer attended. He was still dirty from a day tagging and castrating young bull calves: running each calf from the corral into a squeeze chute until its head came through the gate, his older roommate clamping identification and insecticide tags through their ears, one on each. The ranch's owner, an employer who paid them nothing but a trailer in which to live rent-free, didn't trust the two with the much more precise task of slicing open the bulls' scrotal sacks to cut away their testicles with a scalpel, crouching in the chute behind the young bulls while Art bent the calves' tails up over their backs so that they stood still and would not kick. The rancher did not know that in less than a year's time he will be kicked not by a calf but by his farmhand tenants after telling them he found a buyer for the trailer they lived in, that they were to vacate it within thirty days. And though he will tell them that they were welcome to stay on as regular paid hands, Art and his roommate will protest that they had not been told their quarters were for sale, that they worked hard for their occupancy in it, the argument escalating until they beat the man to the ground in a rage, the heels of their boots breaking his nose, fracturing his eye socket.

The flashlight beam beside Art illuminated the pockmarked marble behind his head, dateless but for raised block letters that read ADAMSON, the inscription *Until Daybreak* etched below. He sat up and passed a near-empty pint bottle of Jack Daniel's to the boy next to him, "Bitch begged me for it."

The boy he passed the bottle to snorted incredulously. "Bullshit," he said. "You probly dug her up from one of these graves. All bony and rotten. Only pussy you ever gonna see."

"You mean your grandma?" Art said, flicking away the butt of his cigarette. He flipped over, humping the earth of the gravesite beneath him, "Fucked her so good I brought her back to life." The other two laughed, the boy Art poked fun at sipping at the bottle of bourbon as though to hide behind it, searching futilely for a comeback. Art righted himself and took up the flashlight, shining it over the weathered headstones and obelisks that surrounded them. "Your granny's walking around here somewhere," he said. He positioned the beam under his chin and altered his voice to sound like Bela Lugosi's Dracula, deep and wavering: "Looking for another young stud to keep her alive." His friends laughed again and Art stood and snatched the bottle away from the boy he had derided. He drank what was left and smashed it against the plump form of a weather-pocked cherub carved into a sepulcher, "I gotta take a leak."

They raced each other through the maze of narrow walkways between vaults and crypts, running toward the creek where it bowed in a wide arc around the old necropolis. The four stood in a row at the edge of a small grassless field kept free of trees and weeds by groundskeepers, pissing over a short shelf of cliff into the water. One of them lost his balance and sat down hard and Art yanked the boy's T-shirt up over his head, kicking him over the bank's edge. The boy rolled down the bank into the shallow water where he thrashed like a fish, his companions laughing and joggling their flashlight beams over him. He knelt upright in drunken confusion, besieged and baffled and struggling to pull his T-shirt back down while the creek flowed around the teen as though he were only a large stone that had tumbled into its midst, its indomitable current blind and insensible of obstructions that in time erode to sediment: wood or stone or flesh-and-bone.

Bitsy turned to the tote bag beside her and lifted the wrapped-up child and laid it beside her. She undid the towel once more, glad not to be able to see well enough to have to look at it again. She pulled the towel out from under the newborn and picked up the naked infant and stood from the bench, walking toward the shadow-shapes of the bushes opposite her. The hills to the east were rimmed with a feeble pink and the girl whimpered quietly at the weak light's prefiguration of dawn, kneeling down to slide the infant underneath a blackberry bush.

The plastic bag rustled along with the rustling of the bush's leaves, Bitsy pushing her arm deep into the barbed vines to place the child where she hoped it would not be seen even in daylight. She winced at the gouging of her knuckles and forearm, knowing those same thorns also cut the child's flesh, the little body catching and snagging as she forced it deeper until she could extend her arm no further. When she pulled back her arm she did so quickly and incautiously, careless of the thorns that tore even more deeply at her skin. She felt the warmth of her own blood and stumbled back to the bench, patting blindly at the planks in search of the towel. Bitsy wrapped her bleeding hand and wondered whether anything could be seen within the snarled mass of blackberry once the sun was up. Then she put the tote bag on the ground and lay down across the bench, her towel-wrapped hand beneath her head like a pillow.

When she awoke it was to a jay's harsh crouping. Bitsy sat up in alarm, not knowing how long she had slumbered. What had before been all but invisible was now cast in meager light, the trees drab green and filled with the spirited chatter of songbirds anticipating sunrise. She looked toward the eastern hills and saw the distinct outline of their peaks, backlit by a pale golden yellow that spotted her eyes when she blinked.

She could see nothing of the infant in the blackberry bush, but the growing light made her anxious of how well she had hidden it. A length of eucalyptus branch lay on the ground beside the tote, now visible in the grayish light, barkless and smooth. Bitsy picked it up and knelt once more beside the blackberry, waving the crooked stick under the bush in search of the child. When she found it she pushed at the body, poking it deeper into the brambles until the branch in her hand suddenly gave no resistance and the girl heard a leafy crash that resounded down the creekbank.

She listened, trying to gauge where the child might land, incredulous of how a thing so small and light could fall in a seemingly endless plummet. When the rustling finally stopped she stood and ran toward the bridge, footsteps clomping loudly over the wood. Bitsy bent over the arched railing, matted hair hanging over her face. She scanned the darkness below but there was nothing to be seen in that tomb of shadow, the creek's quiet babble the only evidence of its being.

The girl let out a cry despite herself, tortured by whether or not the newborn lie in a place light would eventually reveal, by the unutterable things she had done to ensure her child's concealment. Her child. Now that it was lost the idea that the baby was hers occurred to her as it had not before. And it came to her that the infant had no name. But how could it be given one? To name it would be to smother it a second time and wipe away its birth and the girl's and all that had come up to that point in time. The child had been and always would be nameless, its newborn bawl a word before and beyond all words; what all who have ever lived have heard as silence.

Bitsy hung her head over the railing, her face becoming so wet it was as though the stream running under the bridge also ran through her. A drop clung to her chin in a quivering globe that would have shone refractions of sunlight were there sunlight to shine through it. But the arbor kept out the growing dawn. And so in that sequestered dark it dangled at the girl's jaw and then broke and fell, a small soundless splash into the creek below.

She stepped down off the curved bridge the way she had come. The morning sun was higher in the sky, the air tinged with the beginnings of what dry summer heat the day would bring. Bitsy went to the bench and retrieved her tote bag and walked back down the path away from the park toward the shopping center. She saw that the bakery's lights were on, the door open and the outdoor tables and chairs she had seen inside the shop now arranged and ordered along the walkway. A young woman in a white chef's coat stood outside, leaning against one of the windows, smoking. Bitsy smelled fresh bread as she drew closer and felt her stomach grumble. She kept her head down, not wanting to be seen even though she knew she would be unable to pass unnoticed.

"Morning," the woman said cheerily, the double row of buttons on her uniform flashing the rising sunlight in little crescent moons.

Bitsy turned her tear-flushed face and smiled weakly in response, lips pursed upward into a thin line. The girl's eyes were bloodshot, the blue shift she wore dirty and flecked with burrs.

A skin of dry blood stained the insides of her slender legs, flaked and brown like the peeling remnants of sunburn.

The woman's forehead wrinkled and she dropped the butt of her cigarette, grinding it out with the toe of her shoe as she stepped toward Bitsy. "You okay?" she said.

"I'm fine," Bitsy said almost inaudibly, her voice hoarse. She made to hurry on but in her extreme exhaustion could muster no faster pace.

The woman walked beside her, "You sure?" She motioned at the hand Bitsy had wrapped in a towel, "Looks like you hurt yourself."

Bitsy tilted her head down, silent.

"I've got some extra apple Danish today," the woman said, a reserved smile of concern on her face. She moved to stand in front of the girl so that Bitsy was forced to stop. The woman squatted down and looked up in an effort to see Bitsy's downturned, hair-covered face. "You sure you're alright?"

"Yeah. Yes."

The woman reached out and took Bitsy's unbound hand and stood, leading the girl toward a chair. Bitsy let her, too weak and without energy or morale to object, glad to be able to sit down. "Be right back," the woman said. She smiled again but Bitsy made no response, staring at leafy tree designs wrought into the iron tabletop. When the woman returned a moment later she placed a pink box tied with string on the table where the near insensible girl slouched in a daze. She lifted Bitsy's hand and placed a cookie wrapped in waxed paper in her dirty palm, a glazed red berry at its center. "This one's for now," the woman said. She jerked her head toward the box, "You take these Danishes home, okay?"

"Okay," Bisty replied wearily.

"You have a place to take them?"

"Yeah," Bitsy said, getting up, taking the box by its string. "Thank you," she said softly. The woman watched the girl disappear around the corner toward the shopping center walkway and then sat down where Bitsy had been, drawing another cigarette from a pocket and lighting it. She supposed the girl was coming down off drugs, out all Friday night on a high. But then she began to worry that the girl might have been beaten. Or worse. She thought to call the police, unsure if doing so would be unduly meddlesome, remembering the drug-induced things she herself had done in her own recent adolescence until her break time ended and she walked back into the bakery.

Two days later, on Monday, the police will arrive at the bakery to question the woman and the two other bakers that had worked that Saturday, asking about anyone they might have seen during the early morning hours when the shop began baking bread. The woman will remember the swarm of firemen and police in the park that Saturday afternoon, stepping from the bakery to stare along with shoppers and children and curious passers-by, not knowing what the commotion was about. But only an hour before the suited detectives came to the bakery she will have read a story in the county paper. Her heart beat quickly and her mouth became dry as she lied, telling them she had seen no one, relieved at not having told her co-workers about the bedraggled girl that morning for fear the two men would crack vulgar jokes. For days and weeks afterward she will wonder if she had done the right thing, sometimes on the

81

verge of calling the police, her hand on the telephone receiver. She will remember how the girl looked, that spoiled countenance the woman had at the time thought was the face of a teen emerging from a cloud of drugged overindulgence. The woman could not ever bring herself to dial, the single twenty-six-year-old who worked at a bakery carrying her encounter with the girl within her to the end of her days, lavishing attention on her own small boy that Monday afternoon in July of 1980: a child she had not intended but who seemed to shine with a vivacity she appreciated as she had never done before. She watched him pick tiny flowers from the weedy untended grass in her yard and totter to her with them bunched in his dimpled hand and ask what each one was. Dandelion, clover, forget-me-not. When the woman didn't know what they were called she told the boy to invent things to call them and so he did, soon turning his attention from flowers to birds and insects, pointing them out to inscribe them with their new appellations.

Myriad others will have seen the same news story in the county newspaper, then in the local and metropolitan papers, reports that a newborn baby had been suffocated with a plastic bag and tossed down a creekbank. The news item will be read at breakfast tables and on commuter buses, accompanied by sighs and condemnatory remarks and clicking tongues; in diners and in barbers' chairs and at shop counters like the shopping center's variety store where a natty red-faced man in denim work clothes held a copy of that day's local newspaper, chatting about the story with a checker.

"Just can't imagine," the checker said. "Can't understand such an awful thing. It was one of the baggers from the market next door that called the police, you know. One of those little kids who found it brought him right down to that park around back and showed him where it was."

"They find the fiend that did it they'll get the gas chamber," the man replied in a gravelly voice.

"That doesn't seem entirely right to me, Lou. Doesn't seem the decent thing to do."

The red-faced man held up a finger, its nail cracked and dirt-rimmed. "There's no other right thing to do," he carped. "Monsters like them need to settle up in blood."

The checker pursed his lips. "Don't see how that would fix a single thing in this world," he said, shaking his head. "Not a single thing." He turned to the cash register to ring up the man's purchases: detergent, antiseptic wipes, a bar of soap, lye.

The news reports will tell of the discovery by two fifth graders, their names not revealed because of their age. There will be no mention in the news reports of the firefighter-paramedic who scrambled down the creekbank that Saturday afternoon, a man who did not know and would never know that he had seen the infant's mother at the fire station several times: a shy, quiet girl he and his colleagues called "Sodapop." Over the course of his profession he had grown the psychic callus necessary to do his job without letting the horrors of injuries and disfigurements follow him like a phantom, every fatal car accident and heart attack and overdose unnerving him when he'd begun his career until he acclimated and learned to take them in stride. But on very rare occasions that durable psychological casing was pierced as cleanly and precisely as the needles he'd inserted into the countless veins of patients. And so when he kneeled beside the baby in the creekbed he felt like a rookie again, confronting as for the first time what he and others in his line of work had learned to cope with. His practiced detachment buckled as he stared down at the tiny variation of what he had seen so often before, reminded of how ugly and ignominious the deaths he'd witnessed were, whether instant or limping along to arrive after the prolonged loiterings of drawn-out miseries. He remembered treating a young man across the bay years earlier, called to a rough neighborhood just after he'd gone from Intermediate EMT to Paramedic, an event he had not forgotten but which returned with a force of vengeance as though infuriated at having been denied being fully remembered for so long a time. The patient had been a young kid of nineteen or twenty, shot through the neck and perhaps still barely alive when he and his partner arrived after receiving the radio call. A roaring cheer had gone up from the nearby stadium just as he'd inserted a laryngoscope down the youngster's throat, the collective voices of baseball fans at an Athletics game hovering overhead. It was then that he realized he could see straight through the kid's neck: a clear shaft of evening summer sun beaming through the bullet's path as though through the keyhole of a door onto a world of light. Protocol required that he try and bring the boy breath and he and his partner had tried. But each knew they were only going through the motions, that there was nothing to be done. He had been shaken by it, just as he was now shaken by the scratch-scourged newborn in the creekbed, so undeniably deceased protocol did not require any attempt at resuscitation. The firefighter-paramedic knew what many did not: that death was an utterly banal thing; sloppy and plodding and so thoroughly indifferent the only defense against the repeated encounter of such cold was to meet that cold with like aloofness.

His partner arrived moments after he had, knees covered in dirt where he'd slipped negotiating his way down the steep creekbank. "Sweet Jesus," he said, crouching, setting down a bright orange paramedic kit. He opened it, snapping latex gloves over his hands.

"You might as well close that up."

"Yeah," the medic with the soiled knees murmured. "Guess so." He cocked his head. "Why's it all wet?" he said, gazing down at the child in puzzlement over a mystery for which there was no explanation.

A uniformed policeman had asked the boys the same question. Donny looked at Aaron who looked down at his feet, both of them standing in the little park away from the small crowd that had gathered, the aproned, acne-faced teen and the supermarket manager speaking with another officer nearby.

"Washed it off," Aaron said softly. When he was asked why he began to cry, hiding his face in his hands.

Aaron cried again in the back of the police cruiser as he and Donny were driven home, their bicycles retrieved from where they'd been stashed in the V of a double-trunked plum tree near to the ground and placed in the police car's trunk. Aaron felt Donny's hand on his shoulder but the gesture brought him no consolation, only embarrassment, his head turned away toward the window to hide what he could not fight back. He wept just as Bitsy had hours earlier that day, the girl standing at the kitchen sink where morning light shone through the window and sliding glass door, bright on the pink box of pastries she'd set on the counter.

She'd wiped her eyes and stepped out to the balcony feeling hollow and cavernous, regarding the morning brightness as nothing more than day-gloom. Bitsy wondered if rather than at night she'd been conceived during a sunlit hour, wishing it hadn't been at all. She crouched down slowly and sorely and picked up one of her empty Coke bottles and went back inside. She filled it at the faucet and tilted it to her mouth, drinking thirstily as though trying to nurse from the bottle some scrap of comfort. She brought the newly empty bottle into her mother's bedroom and set it on a side table and lay down splay-limbed over the bedspread. Then she fell asleep, not to waken until the late midsummer dusk.

The nearly nine o'clock sunset cast shadows on the girl's apartment complex, shadows that also fell across Aaron's house where the boy lay atop the covers of his parents' bed, his mother beside him stroking his head and fretting over what the police had told her and what her son had told her. For a time the boy had cried in the breathless hiccupping way distressed small children do, upset in a manner his mother thought he had outgrown. Then he quieted and drew a sleeve across his nose and sat up. He looked at her.

"Do you think it got lost?" he asked. "Somebody could have just lost it and then it fell down there."

"Maybe. Maybe it did."

"Why did it have a bag on its head?"

"I don't know, sweetie."

"Donny said vultures could get it."

"I don't think so. They won't now anyway."

"Ants did."

"They won't now."

"Where is it now?"

"They're taking care of it. No ants or vultures. They'll take good care of it."

"What about who lost it?"

"I don't know."

"Will they give it back?"

The boy's mother only wobbled her head vaguely and told the boy to get up and wash his face. She wondered over the questions he had asked and what she had offered, pondering dubious answers for that which was unanswerable, her eyes to the open bedroom window and the fading sunlight there.

That same setting sun dropped below the hills bordering the ranch where Arthur Dolcini and his roommate lounged on the threadbare sofa of the trailer they shared, beer cans in hand, both exhausted from another day of unpaid farm work. "Day like today deserves a little extra, man," Art said, tilting his head back to yawn, his crooked white teeth showing fanglike. "A little something besides free rent. Yesterday was bad enough getting those fuckers de-balled." Art went on about their work with the bull calves the day before and Art's roommate nodded, sipping at his beer. He was employed part-time at an auto parts store where he got Art occasional under-the-table jobs unloading delivery trucks, where they both stole inventory and re-sold it or used the parts on their own cars. He was big and blonde and twenty-one, his eyes close-set and so depthlessly lusterless they resembled those of a stuffed toy. "Like to cut that old turd's nuts off," he said thickly.

"His wife did that a long time ago," Art replied.

The two laughed where they sat on the shabby sofa, joking and drinking, the mild hangover Art had carried with him from the night before at the old historic cemetery slowly soothed away, becoming yet another hangover the next day; a cycle of hangovers and their remedies that would continue until in 2017 Arthur Angelo Dolcini dies one hundred and sixty-six miles north; his liver and kidneys and lungs decayed to ruin. He will listen to the brisk rat-tat of woodpeckers outside amongst the ponderosa pines, the distant barking of a dog. He will see the blurred flash of a swooping jay near the windowpane: a plunging drop of blue sudden and indistinct and an image that will be his mind's eye's last.

Art leaned over to turn on a lamp when the remnants of summer sun no longer came through the trailer's windows, the same fading sunlight still bright on the frosted glass windows of the county coroner's office sixteen miles south, sparkling white-orange fire on its pebbled panes. The body of the child Art did not know and would never know he'd sired lay inside the building, kept in a refrigerated compartment labeled MCC0780-071680. After three hundred and thirteen more sunsets fall over the building the police investigation will close, the case unsolved. The unnamed newborn known only as Baby Doe will be placed in a casket and interred in Valley Memorial Park in May of 1981, a small stainless steel plate punched with a number corresponding to mortuary and county records marking a grave juxtaposed alongside other unknowns buried in earlier times, their simple stone markers reading KNOWN ONLY TO GOD.

Forty-one years later the sun will once more descend, once more among the countless sunsets and sunrises that accompany the passage of those thousands of days, turning the lagoon of an affluent neighborhood of the now much bigger town a rich golden-purple, the houses there built on keys carved out of wetlands adjacent the bay. The woman who had been betrayed by her fiancé and stood at the reservoir's shore fifty-six years earlier will sit on a deck chair with her adult daughter in an early November in 2022, watching the water change color, flocks of marsh wrens swooping in the air above rows of sailboats bobbing alongside their docks.

"Evenfall," the woman said. "It's evenfall. Remember, Susan?"

The woman's daughter looked over at her mother. Her name was Laura.

"Remember that nineteenth century poetry course

we took? The stanza from that Tennyson poem we liked so much. *Maud*, I think it was."

The old woman's daughter sat up in her chair, "Mom?"

"'Alas for her that met me, that heard me softly call,'" the woman recited, "'Came glimmering through the laurels at the quiet evenfall.' Oh that professor was handsome, wasn't he?"

The woman's daughter reached over and placed her hand on her seventy-eight-year-old mother's sweatered arm, "Mom, I'm Laura."

The woman looked down at her daughter's hand and lifted it with her own bony, blue-veined hand, examining the wedding band and the engagement ring Laura wore on the same finger. "How did you get it out!" she exclaimed. "Warren gave me that. How did you get it out of the lake?"

It was the first such instance of confusion Laura would witness, her elderly mother soon after diagnosed with Alzheimer's. The woman became increasingly more befuddled, remembering things from the distant past with clarity but unable to recall the names of common objects or who her grown children were. One afternoon she wandered from the house, spotted by a man walking his dog. He watched the odd spectacle from a distance: a figure bent and white-haired picking her way through the marsh's cord grass and pickleweed toward the creek, the cuffs of her pajama bottoms rolled-up, intent on wading in to search for a ring.

The creek is wide in that flat expanse of wetlands seventeen miles from its origin at the reservoir, freshwater mingling with the salty tide of the bay. A sharp sulfurous tang rises from the marsh's mud where long-necked waterbirds step: herons and white egrets spearing for frogs and snakes and crayfish, devouring their prey in quick guttural swallows. Red-winged blackbirds in yellow-trimmed red epaulets sit atop innumerable cattails, calling a high-pitched *okalee!* in defense of their territories, the birds' perches growing tall in the summer months, home to spiders and wooly orange caterpillars whose cocooned pupae metamorph to emerge as bronze-winged moths. The marshes are bright where the water is still, in places pooled to brackish puddles wherein mosquitoes cluster and angle in the laying of their eggs. East of the green wetlands fields stretch on toward oak-spotted hills: parched and sun-beaten into gold and poised to be set aflame by the merest spark. In autumn the cattails dry out, their long coffee-colored tops breaking to seed in a fluff of white and yellow down and blown away by the wind, landing upon the shallow water, sinking, taking root in the mud beneath; the next year's reeds and leaves gathered up in blackbirds' beaks and woven into nests to cradle their own progeny. In the pre-dawn mornings of winter creatures only dimly lit wade beneath slate-gray skies: long-beaked ghosts amidst the fog and mist, opening enormous white wings that with one brief flap send them airborne, lithe bodies banking over the creek in silent glides, disappearing into the fog as though a part of it.

The creek goes unchanged in its changing, as constant the sky above its many curves and bends, the vultures that circle in that sky. It goes on while Arthur Dolcini and his roommate are arrested on assault and battery charges for beating their landlord, both convicted: Art remanded to a juvenile detention facility, his roommate sentenced to six months in the county jail.

It does not halt for Donald Hogg, caught looking at his father's hidden cache of pornography, his father discomfited more by his son's knowing it was there than for his having seen it. Three years later, a year after Donny's mother is killed in an automobile accident, her car crushed under an eighteen-wheeler and against a concrete median while driving home from a painting class, his father will clear out those concealed magazines along with boxes of his fifteen-year-old son's old threadbare stuffed animals and broken plastic toys and board games, curled and dusty greeting cards, photo albums. Donny will watch while his mother's skirts and dresses and tops—some still in dry cleaners' thin plastic coverings—are brought from his parents' bedroom closet and tossed into a rented Dumpster along with shoes and hair clips and sunglasses and hairbrushes, a blow dryer, boxes of buttons and swaths of fabric, a sewing machine. A fat teenager in a black heavy metal T-shirt emblazoned with the image of a goat's head watching with wet eyes and a pimple-rimmed mouth and refusing to help, that evening climbing into the Dumpster to salvage what his father could not bear to save, hiding the photo albums in the same place the magazines once had been; history becoming a secret thing: hoarded, anonymous, irrevocable.

The creek goes on, one year spilling over its banks during a winter of heavy rains, flooding the town's lowlands and swamping the library near the spot where Donny and Aaron had fixed their eyes on what lay in the creekbed beside an inlet pool; going on even as their friendship fades away, Aaron passing his grade school comrade in the high school's hallways with only the merest trace of acknowledgement. By his senior year Donny will have grown more corpulent and more desperate for friends, the counterfeit brashness masking his loneliness doubly boorish. And so he will be tormented mercilessly, branded with unshakable nicknames: "Hoggy," "Tits," "Hogg Slop." Suddenly befriended by two popular boys, Donny will be persuaded to pull an end-of-the year prank, flattered to have been recruited for an act of sabotage, doing his best to please them. His co-conspirators will stand guard at either end of a hallway after school while Donny goes about his vandal's work: squirting Super Glue in the door locks of a row of classrooms. But when the two lookouts turn occasionally to grin at Donny and then at one another it will be in the knowledge of the greater, crueler prank they had planned: to abandon Hogg Slop before he was finished, timing their departure so that he would be caught in the act by the assistant principal they knew would pass by. The pair will take their seats among the rows of folding chairs assembled on the high school's football field on a Saturday in June 1987. Barred from participating in the ceremony, Donny will watch from the side of a stand of bleachers filled with graduating seniors' friends and families. He will clap and whistle along with them, listening for his name among those read by a teacher at a podium as each robed senior files up to receive their diploma. The name Donald Harris Hogg will not be proclaimed. Donny will draw back and leave the field quietly and gallantly, walking away square-shouldered, his throat constricted. And when he opens the door of his father's car he will hear a cheer go up and turn to see the sky above the football field darken with tasseled mortarboards flung into the air.

It does not stop its course for Elizabeth Eddy who cleans the bathroom on her hands and knees in expectation of her mother's return, Katherine Eddy banging a hip into a doorjamb and cursing boozily, not noticing the bathroom's unusual cleanliness or her daughter's sickness and exhaustion. It goes on after Bitsy's mother marries Rex, a man who proves to be kind and mild and who moves them to another town, a step-father the girl grows to love dearly and who raises Bitsy after her mother runs off with another man. While Bitsy tried on her own graduation robe Rex stood beside her, both of them looking at her reflection in a full-length mirror. He smiled and spoke to her reflection, asking why she looked so glum. When the girl's face crumbled he took his step-daughter's chin in his hand and then embraced her, assuming she mourned the fact that her mother would not be present at her community college commencement. Bitsy thrust her face into his chest, telling him in a burbling rush of choked-off words the thing she had once done on a moonless night before dawn. She spluttered purple-faced and Rex listened with one hand cupped around her head and then began crying along with her, squeezing his step-daughter more tightly and telling her that she was good, she was good, that he loved her and would always love her no matter what, their close-clasped bodies swallowed up by the large robe's billow, faces stark against its dark black sheen.

It goes on for the boy who had first seen Bitsy's child by daylight, Aaron Holiman's temples silvered and his once flat stomach slightly paunched, father to his own children. His identical twin girls will bring home a small fishbowl containing a half dozen tadpoles as a fourth-grade biology project, logging the development of the amphibious larvae for their class. They will feed the dark sperm-shaped creatures pinches of boiled spinach and flakes of hard-boiled egg yolk as they had been instructed. And when one of the tadpoles begins to sprout legs they will proudly show their father, pointing it out from either side of the fishbowl, their small matching faces in unconscious mimic of the other. Images of the creek that summer will open up in him, successive and unbounded like the reflection of one mirror within another: his childhood friend Donny, the magazine, the sun-stippled oak leaves on the creekbank and the entwined branches above that made those sunspots, where they had hidden their bicycles in the low V of a double-trunked plum tree and how the branches of one of its trunks was laden with numberless small purple fruits while the other had none. How he had cried in a police car. The way his friend's thick hand rested on his shoulder. They will return with a potency undiminished in the thirty-four years since he'd been alone with the body of the newborn that afternoon, sitting beside it and seeing himself and the ant-covered infant in the creek's glassy inlet; his face and the image of the child no less true than what lent the water their likenesses.

In time his hair silvers completely, turns white, the thin boy at the creek whose face was patterned with sun and shadow now pleated with wrinkles. He is retired, living in a house fifteen hundred miles from the town he grew up in, his twin girls grown with children of their own. The calendar hangs open to July 2044, the watch on his age-spotted wrist ticking and his wife snoring next to him when a storm comes late at night and all at once. Its hard rain rages in gusts of wind that rattle the windowpanes, branches of the neighbor's tall elm scraping and snapping against the side of the house like the bristles of an enormous twig broom. He wakes at the noise with his face to the half-open window, the thin bedroom curtains ballooning in and then vacuuming out through the sill to flutter outside. Aaron sits up in with his back to the headboard, the suddenly chilled air raising goosebumps on his arms. He watches the curtains move, rapt by the storm's intensity, the rough bangs and clacks of what the brutal wind sweeps down outside, what it tosses and dismantles and carries away. When a brilliant flash strobes through the room his mouth forms a kind of astonished O, everything in the bedroom delivered from darkness in a stark, washed-out whiteness without shadow so that even the inside of his mouth is lit: a ghostlike version of himself glimpsed in a wall mirror. He knows the bolt has struck nearby and tosses off the bedsheets to get up in anticipation of the thunder that will soon follow. But the fierce roar arrives before Aaron can reach his bathrobe hanging on the bedpost: a deep shattering boom that stirs his near-deaf wife; that makes him duck instinctively in defense against a thing from which there is no defense.

Downstairs at the dining room table he sits in the dark, enthralled by the storm's power. He has heard it said that during big summer storms one is to keep all the lights off and never use the telephone. But he would not have turned on lights regardless, not knowing if such precautions reduced the likelihood that lightning would strike a house or if what he'd heard was nothing more than simple folklore passed down through the generations. It is also said that fire can be made from ice if one crafts it like a lens, focusing the sun's rays through it onto tinder. It is said a duck's quack makes no echo. But whatever truth or falsehood there is to such things he does not know. Or care. It is the uncertainness of a storm that has for him its own certainties, unpredictable as they are, unfathomable as they are.

He listens, his shadowed expression lit again in a brief snapshot of alarm at a lightning flare. And then the sharp metallic smell of the air as it gathers in expectation of itself: long seconds before the weighty crack of thunder births. The seventy-five-year-old man adjusts himself in this chair nervously; both restive and thrilled at the mysterious power of something at once everywhere and nowhere.

"What are you doing down here in the dark?"

Aaron turns and sees his wife in the dining room doorway. She clutches closed the lapels of her untied bathrobe with one hand, fiddling to fit her hearing aid into her ear with the other. He does not answer, only holds a crooked finger to his lips as though to say "Shh."

When his wife shakes her head and turns her gaunt figure to go back upstairs, he rises from the table and moves to the enclosed front porch. He winds open the crank windows and breathes the rain's fresh ozone smell through the screens, peers out into the moonless dark. The storm begins to die down and when it passes he can hear the street gutters rushing like dual streams.

He opens the door of his porch and steps barefoot onto rain-wet grass where a litter of storm-blown leaves and twigs lies, fractured branches crisscrossed over one another. And though the yard's foliage is battered and tossed and broken the night is calm and still, as though no storm had ever passed. As a boy he captured tadpoles with a goldfish net and Tupperware container and put them in a kiddie pool in a yard not unlike this one. And when the creatures were forgotten, languishing there untended, devoured by raccoons and skunks, owls and snakes, cannibalized by other tadpoles, the few that remained in the shallow algae-clogged puddle of evaporating water grew larger, growing limbs, finally emerging from the plastic pool. Aquatic things once hatched from eggs born anew. Some emerged by the summer's sun, some during hours of darkness, loping off toward the labyrinthine drapery of honeysuckle vines along the backyard fence, their blossoms' scent more sweetly prominent at night than in daytime; promise of what will be revealed at morning.

The night is warm, the air rain-cleansed. By the light of a nearly burned-out streetlamp the old man can see water roiling up from a storm drain. It is dense and glossy and shines like a liquid pelt, its sound that of a creek in its summertime gurgle. By that gentle sound it tells of its beauty and terribleness, its ceaselessness, of how it is inhabited by forms whose forms are fashioned from that habitation. Like the snake whose figure is made by the shadows its skin's design resembles, spiriting through the yard among the pulsing song of crickets. How many times will it shed its skin, molting a perfect imprint of itself to emerge smooth and newly-scaled? It glides through the grass toward him, over and around fallen branches and scattered twigs, passes silently through his legs. Unable to sleep he stands wide-eyed and awake to the darkness, blades of grass both soft and rough beneath his bare feet, unable to see what is so near him but knowing it is there. At once as baffling and as plainly simple as the faint brief flutter of a moth past his ear.

Acknowledgments

The author wishes to thank the following:
Jessica R. Cadkin to whose love this novella is dedicated—first and foremost and forevermore; Svetlana Lavochkina for her brilliance and selfless advocacy; the Rev. Dr. Kenneth L. Schmidt for his kindness, support, and unfailing friendship; Miette Gillette; Gina Ochsner for her generosity and vision; Kathy Clift & Dan Jackson for invaluable medical advice; Ann Hood; Stephen Wright; Raymond J. Smith†; Edward P. Jones; Kathy Pories; Sylvia Whitman & everyone at Shakespeare and Company; Charles & Clydette de Groot; Erica Wagner; Hala Salah Eldin Hussein; Lionel Minard; Richard L. Thompson; Daniel Kendall, S.J.; James Blaettler, S.J.; my Grandmother Paula Wehrle† & my family; John Roberts; Brian K. Retke; mes frères Dan Golden, Paul K. Miller, & Andrew P. Richard; Evan Harris;

Cameron V. Blackwell; Stefanino Lancellotta; St. Ignatius Parish; the Oakland Writers' Notto, especially Lisa Margonelli & Mary Roach; the Center for Religious Humanism; the Center for Cultural Innovation; the Novato Public Library.

AMDG

About the Author

Agustín Maes was born in New Mexico where his ancestors settled in the 1630s and grew up in California thirty miles north of San Francisco. In 2011, *Newborn* was chosen as a runner-up for the Paris Literary Prize, sponsored by Shakespeare and Company and the de Groot Foundation. His work has been published in *The Gallatin Review*, *Blue Mesa Review*, *Ontario Review*, *Turnrow*, *The Other Journal*, anthologized in *New Stories from the South: The Year's Best*, and cited in *The Best American Mystery Stories*. His work has also been translated into French, and into Arabic for *Albawtaka Review*, an Egyptian quarterly. He graduated from the San Francisco Art Institute and holds an MFA from the New School in New York and an MA from the University of San Francisco. Maes was the

2009-2010 Milton Fellow at Seattle Pacific University. He resides in Oakland, California.

About the Publisher

Whisk(e)y Tit is committed to restoring degradation and degeneracy to the literary arts. We work with authors who are unwilling to sacrifice intellectual rigor, unrelenting playfulness, and visual beauty in our literary pursuits, often leading to texts that would otherwise be abandoned in today's largely homogenized literary landscape. In a world governed by idiocy, our commitment to these principles is an act of civil service and civil disobedience alike.